This book is dedicat
brothers Jason and Nick Meyer.
As I remember, we were
ALWAYS nice to each other.

Title ID: 6201984

ISBN-13: 978-1532705908
ISBN-10: 1532705905

Three Nice Mice

WRITTEN and ILLUSTRATED
by Lori Ehlke

Three nice mice.
Three nice mice.
See how nice they are.
See how nice they are.

They're **always** polite when they nibble their cheese.

They never forget to say "Thank you" and "Please".

They cover their noses whenever they sneeze.

AH, AH, AH...

Three nice mice.

Three nice mice.

See how nice they are.

See how nice they are.

They play with their friends and remember to **share**.

They wait for their turn, and they try to be **fair**.

They cheer for their teammates to show that they care.

HIP, HIP, HIP

Three nice mice.

Three nice mice.

Three nice mice.

Three nice mice.

See how nice they are.

See how nice they are.

They say, "Please **excuse me**," and don't interrupt.

They **play** with their toys and then pick them all up.

TOYS

They like to use kind words to build others up.

YOU ARE THE

Three Nice Mice

Music and Chords

Three nice mice. Three nice mice. See how nice they are. See how nice they

are. They're al - ways po - lite when they ni - bble their cheese. They
They play with their friends and re - mem - ber to share. They
They say, "Please ex - cuse me," and don't in - ter - upt. They

ne - ver for - get to say thank you and please. They co - ver their no - ses when
wait for their turn and they try to be fair. They cheer for their team-mates to
play with their toys and then pick them all up. They like to use kind words to

ev - er they sneeze. Ah ah ah CHOOO! Three nice mice. Three nice mice
show that they care. Hip hip hip HOORAY!
build o-thers up. You are the BEST!

Hand Actions:

Three nice mice. Three nice mice. (Hold up 3 fingers)

See how nice they are. See how nice they are. (Hold your hand above your eyes)

They're always polite when they nibble their cheese. (Pretend to nibble cheese)

They never forget to say thank you and please. (Shake finger back and forth side to side)

They cover their noses whenever they sneeze. (Cover your nose with your elbow)

AH, AH, AH CHOOO! (Pretend to sneeze)

Three nice mice. Three nice mice. (Hold up 3 fingers)

About the Author

Lori Ehlke writes books, paints pictures, makes music, teaches art classes, travels, and goes on adventures. She learned to teach at Martin Luther College, learned to paint in Florence, Italy, and learns more about children every day as she and her husband raise their four kids.

"Three Nice Mice" was inspired by growing up with her twin brothers. Just as Lori's parents tried to instill good manners in her and her brothers, now Lori tries to do the same with her children. Lori has to work on her own good manners, however, when sharing chocolate is involved!

You can also check out Lori's first book, "Bless this Mess", about the chaos that twin babies can add to a house.   It is available on Amazon.
See more of Lori's work at WWW.LORIEHLKE.NET or on "Lori Ehlke's Art" Facebook page.

Photo credit: Scott Glenn

Made in the USA
Lexington, KY
21 December 2017